An Early Chapter Book

ADAPTED BY CATHERINE HAPKA

HarperEntertainment
An Imprint of HarperCollins*Publishers*

TM & © 2002 Twentieth Century Fox Film Corporation. All rights reserved.
Printed in the United States of America. No part of this book may be used or
reproduced in any manner whatsoever without written permission except in the
case of brief quotations embodied in critical articles and reviews. For information
address HarperCollins Publishers Inc., 10 East 53rd Street, New York, NY 10022.

HarperCollins books are available at special quantity discounts
for bulk purchases for sales promotions, premiums, or fund-raising
For information please call or write:
Special Markets Department, HarperCollins Publishers Inc.,
10 East 53rd Street, New York, NY 10022.
Telephone: (212) 207-7528. Fax: (212) 207-7222.

ISBN 0-06-093814-5

HarperCollins®, 👑 ®, and HarperEntertainment™ are trademarks
of HarperCollins Publishers Inc.

First printing: February 2002

Visit HarperEntertainment on the World Wide Web at
www.harpercollins.com

10 9 8 7 6 5 4 3 2

CHAPTER ONE

"Oh, look at the cute little baby, Diego!"

I looked. When Soto tells you to do something, you do it.

The two of us were crouched on the ridge watching the human camp. I saw a tiny, soft, pink creature lift its pudgy front limbs and totter for a second on its hind feet, trying to find its balance. Then it toppled to the ground. Its parents laughed and cooed as they watched.

"Isn't it nice the baby will be joining us for dinner," Soto commented.

"It's the least we can do," I said.

My tail twitched nervously as I watched the two-legged creatures below. We saber-toothed tigers get along just fine with most other predators. They don't bother us; we don't bother them. But humans are different. They poach our prey, hunt our pack, and use our skins to keep warm.

"Especially when his daddy wiped out half our pack and scouts our territory with a baby," Soto snarled, narrowing his eyes at the baby's father, the leader of the human pack. "A *baby*, Diego. It's downright disrespectful, don't you think?"

"Let's show Daddy what happens when he messes with a saber," I snarled.

"Alert the troops," Soto growled. "We attack at dawn."

I nodded and turned to go.

"And, Diego, bring me that baby"— Soto told me sharply—"alive. If I'm going to enjoy my revenge I want it to be fresh."

I heard the others talking as I approached. Oscar was muttering about Soto's obsession with humans while Zeke and Lenny were whining about the migration.

The migration. I paused, thinking about it. Creatures of all shapes and sizes were moving south—plump aardvarks, tasty little scrats, crunchy glyptodons. For a saber-toothed tiger, the migration was a walking buffet. And I knew my packmates were hungry. My own stomach was growling like Soto in a bad mood. I pushed those thoughts aside and hurried forward.

"Listen up," I told the others. I was proud to be Soto's messenger. It meant that he trusted me. "We attack the humans at dawn."

"Aw, no," Zeke sputtered.

"There's no meat on a human," Lenny added.

I frowned. When pack members start questioning Soto's orders, everyone ends up in trouble. "There won't be any meat on you either if you don't do what Soto says," I warned them.

When dawn came, we were ready. The human camp was still. The fires were almost out. The only ones who heard us coming were the wolves who hung around the human camp. But we were already running into the camp by the time their barking woke the humans.

As the others attacked, I crept into the human leader's tent. The baby, Roshan, was sleeping inside. I lifted the tiny creature gently, being careful not to hurt it with my sharp teeth. Soto would be angry if it was damaged.

I peered out of the tent flap. Now all I had to do was sneak past the fighting and get back to our—

Whack!

"Aaaaargh!" I yowled in pain. Whirling around, I saw Roshan's mother, Nadia. She dropped her club, grabbed the baby, and ran.

My head was spinning, but I knew I had to follow. I didn't want to face Soto's anger if I lost his prize.

I raced after the human woman. Her two legs were no match for my four. I caught up to her just outside of camp,

at the edge of a cliff overlooking a
waterfall. She had nowhere to run.

Still, Nadia refused to give up. I
was surprised at her courage. Even
when I swiped at her, trying to snag
the baby, she refused to give up. I
shook my paw, distracted for a moment
as Roshan's bead necklace caught on
one claw.

At that moment Nadia turned—and leaped off the cliff! Stunned, I leaned over the edge as she tumbled through the air, Roshan still in her arms.

I wasn't sure what to do. Should I go down the cliff after the baby? Was it still alive? Would Soto still want it? I just didn't know.

Soto spotted me as I returned to the scene of the battle. "There's Diego!" he howled. "Fall back!"

When he asked about the baby, I took a deep breath. "I lost it over the falls," I said.

Lenny, Zeke, and Oscar started moaning and complaining, but I had ears only for Soto. "I want that baby, Diego," he said, his voice cold.

"I'll get it," I promised.

"You'd better," Soto growled. "We'll go up to Half-Peak—meet us there. And, Diego, you'd better hope it's alive!"

I gulped and nodded. I knew what I had to do.

CHAPTER TWO

It was a long, steep, rocky climb down the cliff wall. The whole time I kept hearing Soto's voice: *You'd better hope he's alive.*

Would the baby be alive? Humans seemed so easy to break, with their awkward limbs and smooth pink skin. I hoped Roshan was stronger than he looked.

Near the bottom I peered over a rock, hoping to spot the baby. "Huh?" I muttered as a strange sight met my eyes.

Standing beside the river was a huge woolly mammoth. A smaller creature was there, too—a sloth. And the sloth was holding the human baby!

What was going on? I crouched out of sight to listen. The two creatures seemed to be arguing about Roshan.

"You're an embarrassment to nature, you know that?" the mammoth said, sounding disgusted.

The sloth muttered something and turned toward the cliff.

Clutching the baby, he started to climb. He managed to hoist himself a short way up the wall. The mammoth watched. I still couldn't figure out what the two of them were doing. Mammoths and sloths don't usually hang out together.

It didn't really matter, though. The important thing was getting the baby. The sloth was struggling over another boulder. I noticed Roshan's pelt loosening. This could be my chance—

I tensed my muscles. The pelt slipped. The sloth struggled to keep hold of the baby but lost his grip. I leaped out of my hiding place as Roshan plummeted toward the rocky ground.

Aha! I caught him in my teeth, landing neatly on a rock.

Whack!

My head exploded in pain—again. Before I could react, a huge, hairy trunk snaked forward and grabbed the baby from me.

"That pink thing is mine!" I cried.

"Ah, no," the sloth said. "That pink thing belongs to us."

"'Us'?" I repeated. "You two are an odd couple."

The mammoth frowned at the sloth. "There is no us."

I decided to try the friendly approach. "The baby?" I wheedled. "Please? I was returning it to its herd."

"Yeah, nice try, bucktooth," the sloth said.

This wasn't going to be easy. The sloth, Sid, was all talk—he would be no match for my teeth and claws on his own. But the mammoth, Manfred, seemed to be protecting him. I couldn't figure out why, since the two of them didn't even seem to like each other.

I followed as they climbed toward the human camp. They seemed surprised to see it deserted. I wasn't surprised. I knew the humans had rushed off to find Soto and the others.

"They couldn't be far." Sid looked around helplessly. "They went this way.

Or this way." He scratched his head. "Or maybe . . . hmmm . . ."

"You don't know much about tracking, do you?" I commented. I saw my chance to get Roshan out of their grasp.

Sid shrugged. "Hey, I'm a sloth—see a tree, eat a leaf. That's my tracking."

I turned to Manfred. "You didn't miss them by much." I showed him a broken branch. "They headed north two hours ago."

I hoped Manfred would give me the baby to return. Instead, he announced that he and Sid would return him to the humans themselves—and that I would lead the way.

It wasn't exactly the plan I had in mind. But I figured things could still work out. When Manfred moved out of earshot for a second, I circled Sid.

"You won't always have Jumbo around to protect you," I hissed.

Sid looked nervous, and I smiled. This might take a little longer than expected. But I planned to take that baby to Soto in triumph.

No matter what.

CHAPTER THREE

Human babies may be small, but they can make a big noise.

"You gotta make it stop," Manfred moaned. "I can't take it anymore."

It was only hours into their journey, but it felt like days to them.

Sid was holding the baby. "It won't stop squirming," he complained.

"You're holding it wrong!" I snapped.

Manfred ordered Sid to check the baby's diaper. Sid peeled it back.

"Eew, yuck, eew!" Sid held the dirty pelt in the air.

"Stop waving that thing around!" I warned him, wrinkling my nose. Human babies can make a big stink, too.

Sid tripped, and the dirty pelt flew out of his grasp—right into Manfred's face.

"Eew! Yuck!" Manfred cried.

Sid laughed. But Manny didn't. He stared Sid down then bopped him on the head. The baby finally stopped crying for a second —and giggled.

I blinked at him in amazement. Sid and Manfred stopped what they were doing and stared.

The baby started crying again. Manfred bonked Sid again, and once more the baby laughed.

"Hey, do that again," I told them. "He likes it!"

Manfred whacked Sid again. "Yeah," he said happily. "It's making me feel better, too."

Unfortunately, that only worked for a little while. Then I had an idea. Peekaboo! That always amused tiger cubs.

I smiled at the yowling baby. "Where's the baby?" I uncovered my eyes and flashed my

biggest toothy grin at him. "There he is!"
This was fun. I tried again. "Where's the
baby? There he is!"

The baby watched me, his eyes wide. For a second I thought it was working. Then he started bawling louder than ever.

Manfred shoved me aside. "Stop it," he said, grabbing the baby. "You're scaring him." I guess my razor-sharp three-foot-long teeth frightened the little fellow.

I was a little insulted, but I let it pass. Sid tried to figure out what to do next. Manfred was too busy trying to soothe Roshan to help.

Then Manny said something that got everyone's attention—"Food!"

He pointed in the direction of a dodo marching past. I frowned. Dodos aren't food. They're too small to make even a light snack.

Then I saw what Manny had really been pointing to—a melon! Manny picked it up, but as fast as lightning the dodo grabbed it and rolled it right past us, getting away before we really knew what happened. Sid started chasing the bird, with Manfred and me close behind. The dodo led us right to a huge dodo camp.

Manfred walked up to the dodo leader. "Hey, can we have our melon back?" he asked. "Junior's hungry." He pointed to the baby.

The dodos all started chattering wildly. They didn't want to share their food. But being dodos, they messed up —and kicked a melon right at us.

That caused a big ruckus.

"The baby," I thought. "Now is my chance."

I looked around to be sure no one was watching me.

But before I could make a move toward the baby, something happened

that grabbed everyone's attention. The dodos managed to escape—right over the edge of a cliff!

Roshan happily slurped melon.

"I give that species 40,000 years," I said. "Tops."

We headed into the mountains. I'd missed my chance to grab the baby this time. But I knew there would be another chance. Maybe tonight, after my new friends were—

Wait a minute. I stopped myself in mid-thought. Had I really just thought of bossy Manfred and annoying Sid as . . . as . . . *friends*?

I shook my head. The baby's smelly diapers were going to my brain, I figured. No way were those pathetic creatures friends of mine.

And tonight, as soon as they fell asleep, Roshan and I would be out of there.

CHAPTER FOUR

Sid and the baby fell asleep right away. But I thought Manfred would never close his eyes. He kept staring at me as I pretended to sleep.

Finally, though, his eyes drooped shut. A moment later he was snoring. Carefully, not making a sound, I crept toward Manfred and the baby. Closer. Closer. Closer . . .

Snap!

A twig cracked nearby. I froze.

Snap!

Louder this time. Manfred didn't wake up, but his trunk tightened around Roshan.

Grr! Whoever was snapping twigs back in the brush had ruined my chance! And that creature was going to pay . . . I crouched low, stalking the source of the sound. The leaves rustled just ahead. I pounced.

A tiger! I'd tackled another saber-tooth. Zeke!

"I'm working here!" I snarled at him angrily.

Oscar appeared from the brush. "Tracking down helpless infants too difficult for you?" He sneered at me. "Soto's getting tired of waiting."

"Yeah," Zeke added. "He said: Come back with the baby or don't come back at all."

I winced. I knew Soto. Even if I brought the baby to him now, he might think it was too late.

I had to do something to prove myself. "I have a message for Soto," I said coolly. "Tell him I'm bringing the baby. And tell him I'm bringing . . . a mammoth."

I showed them the sleeping Manfred.
They were ready to attack that very
moment. But I stopped them.

"Not yet!" I warned. "We'll need the
whole pack to bring this mammoth
down."

The next day I couldn't stop thinking
about my talk with Zeke and Oscar.
Could it be my promise that was
bothering me—the promise to deliver
Manfred to the pack?

I was distracted, as usual, by Sid's
goofing around. He managed to disappear

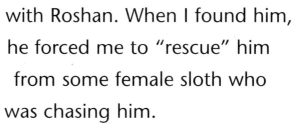

with Roshan. When I found him, he forced me to "rescue" him from some female sloth who was chasing him.

It was tempting just to chomp him and be done with it. But I played along so we could keep moving.

By midday we were crossing a glacier field. When I jumped on a rock to find our path, I spotted something moving in the valley below—the humans! I had to stop the others from seeing them, or my plan would be ruined. So would my life. Soto would never forgive me if I failed now.

"Great news!" I called. "I found a shortcut." I pointed out a crevice in the ice. It would take us away from the humans—and toward the tiger trap that was waiting for Manfred.

"Through there?" Manfred sounded worried.

"No thanks," Sid added. "I choose life."

I was losing patience with his goofy comments. "Move, sloth!" I thundered.

My shout echoed loudly. Too loudly. It started an avalanche.

"Quick! Inside!" I yelped. We raced through the crevice into a series of caves.

Roshan crawled away and slid down an ice tunnel. We went after him and ended up skidding through a whole series of tunnels and slides. It was so cool I wanted to go again. But I knew I shouldn't be having so much fun because, after all, I was leading them into a trap.

When we landed, we found ourselves
in a huge cavern with paintings of animals
and humans on the walls.

"Look!" Sid said. "Tigers!"

Sure enough, some saber-toothed tigers
were among the creatures in the painting.
Next Sid pointed out a mammoth.

He moved closer to the picture. "Hey, this
fat one looks like you," he told Manfred.
"Aw, he's got a family."

Manfred moved closer. As Sid babbled on
about the baby mammoth, I noticed that
Manfred was staring at the picture. His face
was sad.

Suddenly it all made sense. That was why Manfred was traveling alone. And why he wanted to help the human baby. He'd lost his own baby.

"Sid," I said to the sloth, who was still chattering away. "Shut up."

Sid looked at Manfred and finally got it. "Oh."

Manfred didn't seem to remember that the rest of us were there—not until Roshan patted the picture of the baby mammoth. Then Manfred picked him up, and we turned to go.

I paused, looking back curiously. What had happened to Manfred's family? I would probably never know. But I couldn't help seeing Manfred in a whole new way. It made it harder than ever to imagine leading him into Soto's waiting jaws. . . .

I snapped out of those thoughts when Sid started complaining about his sweaty feet. I realized my feet were warm, too. Then—

Boom!

CHAPTER FIVE

Boom! Boom! Boom!

Lava exploded all around us.

"Run!" we all yelled at once.

The ground was bubbling and falling away everywhere I looked.

Within seconds,
the only safe ground
was a few narrow,
dangerous-looking
bridges of ice. Below
were deadly rivers of lava.

"Don't look down!" Manfred warned.

"I looked!" Sid yelped in terror.

Crack!

The section of ice between me and Sid
suddenly dropped away. I found myself
on a tiny platform of ice.

I leaped forward,
landing
on the
larger
ice
bridge
with Sid
and Manfred.

"Wow!" Sid said. "I wish I could jump like that."

"Wish granted," Manfred said, punting him across the gap onto safe ground on the far side.

Meanwhile I was stuck behind Manfred. I could hear popping and sizzling and cracking all around. Any second now the heat would melt the bridge, and we would

all be part of the lava soup below. If
I was alone, I would be on the other
side by now. But Manfred was big—he
couldn't move that fast.

"Move faster!" I urged him nervously.

Crack!

A section of ice dropped in front of
Manfred. He leaped—landing safely on
the far side.

I was relieved. But only for a second.

I noticed the ice beneath me melting fast. It was now or never. I leaped—but my paw slipped on the ice, and I scrabbled for a hold on the edge of the broken bridge.

"Diego!" Sid cried.

Manfred moved back onto the bridge and edged toward me. I struggled to hold on. But I slipped and lost my grip.

I closed my eyes, waiting to feel the burning lava. Instead I felt a strong trunk grab my leg. Manfred!

He hurled me toward the ledge. I landed safely— just as the ice broke, sending Manfred tumbling out of sight!

"Manny!" Sid screamed.

Ka-boom!

Suddenly Manfred came shooting up, carried by an explosion of rock and lava. He landed on the ledge beside us with a thud.

He was okay! I couldn't believe it. I also couldn't believe he'd almost given his own life to save mine.

"Why did you do that?" I asked him.

Manfred shrugged. "That's what you do in a herd. You look out for each other."

"I don't know about you, but we're the weirdest herd I've ever seen," said Sid.

I had to admit that Sid was right. We were a herd. In the tiger pack it was every animal for itself. No one would help you out, ever. This herd sure was different.

We moved on, stopping for the night on a mountain summit. Sid even built a fire.

Then it happened. Roshan pushed
himself up—and stood on his two hind
legs. He staggered along, heading straight
for me—

And fell,
hugging my
front paw.

As I stared
down at the
little guy, so
pink and
helpless
and small,
I suddenly knew I couldn't do it. I couldn't
lead Manfred and Sid into that trap.
Instead, I had to help them return the
baby to his family.

I lifted Roshan to his feet. This would mean the end of life with my old pack. The end of being Soto's favorite. But that didn't matter so much all of a sudden. Because now I was part of a herd.

My new friends.